WOMEN & RELIGION
Reinterpreting Scriptures
to Find the Sacred Feminine

RELIGION & MODERN CULTURE
Title List

WOMEN & RELIGION
Reinterpreting Scriptures to Find the Sacred Feminine

by Kenneth R. McIntosh, M.Div.

Mason Crest Publishers
Philadelphia

Mason Crest Publishers Inc.
370 Reed Road
Broomall, Pennsylvania 19008
(866) MCP-BOOK (toll free)

First printing
1 2 3 4 5 6 7 8 9 10

Library of Congress Cataloging-in-Publication Data

McIntosh, Kenneth, 1959–
  Women & religion : reinterpreting Scriptures to find the sacred feminine / by Kenneth R. McIntosh.
      p. cm. — (Religion and modern culture)
  Includes bibliographical references and index.
  ISBN 1-59084-977-9 1-59084-970-1 (series)
  1. Women and religion—Juvenile literature. 2. Feminism—Religious aspects—Juvenile literature. I. Title: Women and religion. II. Title. III. Series.
  BL458.M39 2005
  200'.82—dc22
                                      2005017175

Produced by Harding House Publishing Service, Inc.
www.hardinghousepages.com
Interior design by Dianne Hodack.
Cover design by MK Bassett-Harvey.
Printed in India.

CONTENTS

INTRODUCTION

by Dr. Marcus J. Borg

You are about to begin an important and exciting experience: the study of modern religion. Knowing about religion—and religions—is vital for understanding our neighbors, whether they live down the street or across the globe.

Despite the modern trend toward religious doubt, most of the world's population continues to be religious. Of the approximately six billion people alive today, around two billion are Christians, one billion are Muslims, 800 million are Hindus, and 400 million are Buddhists. Smaller numbers are Sikhs, Shinto, Confucian, Taoist, Jewish, and indigenous religions.

Religion plays an especially important role in North America. The United States is the most religious country in the Western world: about 80 percent of Americans say that religion is "important" or "very important" to them. Around 95 percent say they believe in God. These figures are very different in Europe, where the percentages are much smaller. Canada is "in between": the figures are lower than for the United States, but significantly higher than in Europe. In Canada, 68 percent of citizens say religion is of "high importance," and 81 percent believe in God or a higher being.

The United States is largely Christian. Around 80 percent describe themselves as Christian. In Canada, professing Christians are 77 percent of the population. But religious diversity is growing. According to Harvard scholar Diana Eck's recent book *A New Religious America*, the United States has recently become the most religiously diverse country in the world. Canada is also a country of great religious variety.

Fifty years ago, religious diversity in the United States meant Protestants, Catholics, and Jews, but since the 1960s, immigration from Asia, the Middle East, and Africa has dramatically increased the number of people practicing other religions. There are now about six million Muslims, four million Buddhists, and a million Hindus in the United States. To compare these figures to two historically important Protestant denominations in the United States, about 3.5 million are Presbyterians and 2.5 million are Episcopalians. There are more Buddhists in the United States than either of these denominations, and as many Muslims as the two denominations combined. This means that knowing about other religions is not just knowing about people in other parts of the world—but about knowing people in our schools, workplaces, and neighborhoods.

Moreover, religious diversity does not simply exist between religions. It is found within Christianity itself:

• There are many different forms of Christian worship. They range from Quaker silence to contemporary worship with rock music to traditional liturgical worship among Catholics and Episcopalians to Pentecostal enthusiasm and speaking in tongues.

- Christians are divided about the importance of an afterlife. For some, the next life—a paradise beyond death—is their primary motive for being Christian. For other Christians, the afterlife does not matter nearly as much. Instead, a relationship with God that transforms our lives this side of death is the primary motive.
- Christians are divided about the Bible. Some are biblical literalists who believe that the Bible is to be interpreted literally and factually as the inerrant revelation of God, true in every respect and true for all time. Other Christians understand the Bible more symbolically as the witness of two ancient communities—biblical Israel and early Christianity—to their life with God.

Christians are also divided about the role of religion in public life. Some understand "separation of church and state" to mean "separation of religion and politics." Other Christians seek to bring Christian values into public life. Some (commonly called "the Christian Right") are concerned with public policy issues such as abortion, prayer in schools, marriage as only heterosexual, and pornography. Still other Christians name the central public policy issues as American imperialism, war, economic injustice, racism, health care, and so forth. For the first group, values are primarily concerned with individual behavior. For the second group, values are also concerned with group behavior and social systems. The study of religion in North America involves not only becoming aware of other religions but also becoming aware of differences within Christianity itself. Such study can help us to understand people with different convictions and practices.

And there is one more reason why such study is important and exciting: religions deal with the largest questions of life. These questions are intellectual, moral, and personal. Most centrally, they are:

- What is real? The religions of the world agree that "the real" is more than the space-time world of matter and energy.
- How then shall we live?
- How can we be "in touch" with "the real"? How can we connect with it and become more deeply centered in it?

This series will put you in touch with other ways of seeing reality and how to live.

Chapter 1

RELIGION & MODERN CULTURE

WOMEN & MODERN SPIRITUALITY

Katlyn attends a Southern Baptist Church, along with her parents and little brother. She knows the preacher at her church will always be a male, as will the youth pastor and other leaders. She also knows how things work in her family: Dad is clearly head of their household, and if she needs permission to take the car or wants a bigger allowance, Katlyn knows better than to ask Mom—her mother will only pass the decision to Dad. Her parents and teachers believe male leadership at home and in the church is a pattern God established in the Bible.

Yet Katlyn watches television, where she sees female detectives solving cases on *CSI*, a woman running the counterterrorism unit on *24*, and countless other examples of women whose intelligence and talents enable them to work as equals with men. She also gets better grades than most of her classmates who are male. Privately, she wonders: *If women can do all these things, does God really want men to make all the decisions in the church and family?*

Ashley sits with her family in the pews at Knox Presbyterian Church. Pastor Sally is preaching, as she does every Sunday. Ashley remembers when she was a little girl and Pastor Sally replaced Pastor Tom; some members of the church opposed a woman pastor. It has been years now since Ashley heard any complaints about a woman pastor because Pastor Sally does a great job—she preaches interesting sermons, visits church members faithfully, and even started a weekly soup kitchen for the homeless.

Recently, Ashley was eating in the school cafeteria and chatting with Jared, who is known as a "born again" Christian. When she quoted Pastor Sally, Jared gave her a funny look and said, "You do realize that God's Word forbids women preachers." Ashley didn't realize, in fact she thought maybe Jared was pulling her leg, but he pulled a worn Bible from his backpack and read to her from the Apostle Paul's letter to Timothy, "I do not permit a woman to teach or have authority over a man." The conversation left Ashley confused; she was not sure what to think about Jared, the Bible, or her church.

Rachel does not regard herself as part of any major religion. Her mom raised her with good morals, but church or synagogue has never been part of their lives. Rachel has been exploring religion on the Internet, chatting with various people about their beliefs. She feels drawn to **Pagan** and Goddess sites because they offer a spirituality that affirms women and nature. Rachel always wondered why the Divine Being

GLOSSARY

evangelical: Relating to any Protestant Christian church whose members believe in the authority of the Bible and salvation through acceptance of Jesus Christ as personal savior.

Pagan: Having to do with religions outside the world's main religions, that often emphasize the Earth and the Goddess.

sexism: Discrimination against men or women because of their sex.

should be a "he" instead of "she," so Goddess spirituality makes sense to her. At the same time, she occasionally goes with friends to their churches and synagogues. She finds organized religion interesting, but her real affinity—at least for now—is with Mother Earth.

WOMEN'S SPIRITUALITY & POPULAR CULTURE

At the start of the twenty-first century, people of faith are asking questions about the roles of women in religion. The women's rights movement was one of the greatest changes in North America during the nineteenth and twentieth centuries. For thousands of years, men could buy, sell, beat, marry, and impregnate women against the women's wishes,

"Feminist perspectives have often criticized various religions for their treatment of women. They are absolutely right. Illustrations of religious abuse of females can be pointed out in the United States and internationally. What many feminist perspectives don't take into account is that Jesus would have been one of feminism's greatest allies."

—*Marilyn Adamson, from EveryStudent.com*

giving them no opportunity to choose a career or a role in politics. Over two centuries, the feminist movement in North America made enormous strides. While **sexism** is still a challenge, fewer people in the United States or Canada are willing to admit sexist views. Women have moved into all professions, at least to some degree, and sex discrimination is mostly illegal. However, attitudes questioning sexual equality still exist in North America—especially in religion. What does the Bible say about women in religion? Is God male, female, or neither? How can women practice religion in a way that honors them?

Some Christian denominations, including the Roman Catholic Church, Greek Orthodox Church, and Southern Baptist Church, along with Orthodox Jewish synagogues, Mormon churches, and Muslim mosques, teach that God limits women's roles in religion. Some women are content within these traditions, while others are not. Some other Christian churches, including the United Methodist, Episcopal, Presbyterian Church USA, and American Baptists, along with Reformed Judaism, interpret the Bible in ways that support women's equality in church, family, and society. These interpreters are convinced that the Bible itself supports women's full equality with men. There are also North American citizens who believe Christianity and Judaism are

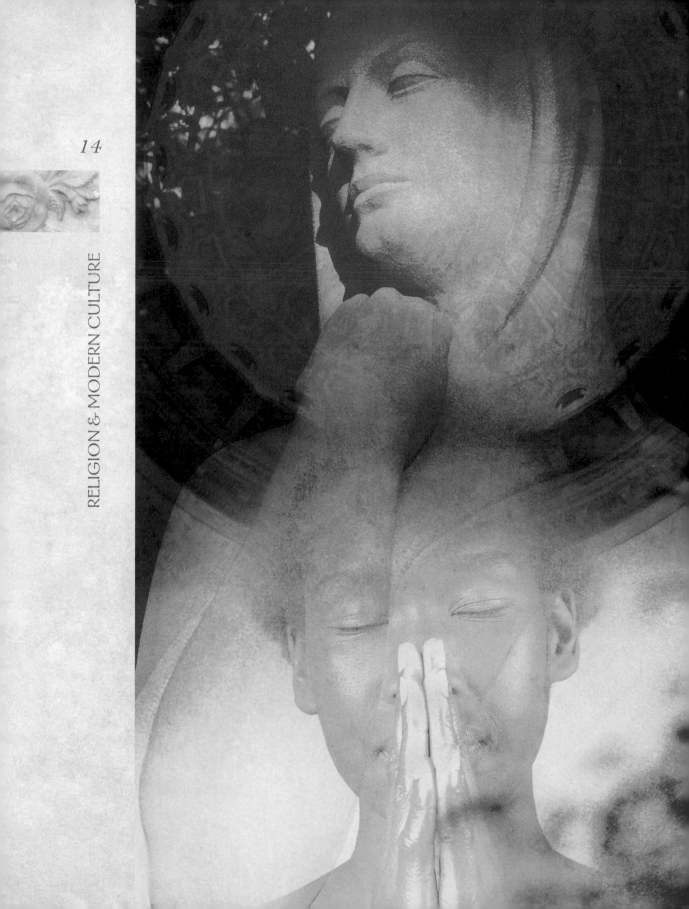

RELIGION & MODERN CULTURE

THREE DIFFERING APPROACHES TO WOMEN'S SPIRITUALITY IN THE TWENTY-FIRST CENTURY

1. Accept or embrace traditional religious teachings that differentiate men's and women's roles (for example, male leadership, women as homemakers).
2. Reinterpret the scriptures and traditions of the major religions to allow female leadership and feminine understanding of God.
3. Revive Goddess religions as feminist alternatives.

incurably sexist. Some persons committed to feminism and ecology have revived traditions honoring the Goddess and Mother Earth.

Discussions about women's roles in religion are by no means limited to church or temple, as popular culture also explores these issues. Dan Brown's novel *The Da Vinci Code* has sold more than 17 million copies. In this novel, French code expert Sophie Neveu and American professor Robert Langdon must avoid the French police and a Catholic Church assassin while investigating mysterious clues in the paintings of Leonardo da Vinci. In this fictional story, they discover a hidden truth: Mary Magdalene was the bride of Jesus Christ, and there is a carefully guarded bloodline of their descendants to this day. While the novel angers some Christians with its attacks on treasured beliefs such as Christ's divinity, *The Da Vinci Code* appeals to many readers who, like the novel's heroes, are pursuing a female image of the Divine.

Worship of the Goddess in the form of Wicca is also a growing popular phenomenon. Books like *Teen Witch* by Silver RavenWolf and *Witchin: A Handbook for Teen Witches* by Fiona Horne are popular with teens. Television shows like *Charmed*, with its trio of glamourous model-looking witches, and *Buffy the Vampire Slayer*, with Buffy's Wiccan sidekick Willow, have helped to popularize Wicca.

There is another movement today urging a return to traditional sex roles. Popular author John Eldredge, materials by Focus on the Family, and publications of the Mormon and Southern Baptist churches warn that feminism may erode families; they urge women to embrace traditional roles (for example, motherhood, submission to husbands, acceptance of male religious leaders). Women produce some of these materials, and many women within conservative religious groups say they prefer traditional roles.

SCHOLARS DEBATE WOMEN'S ROLES IN THE SCRIPTURES & RELIGIOUS TRADITIONS

While books and movies may influence ordinary people, churches and temples look to their trained experts for guidance on the pressing issues of the day. Were there women priests in the early Christian church? What influence did Mohammed's wives have on the religious life of the Prophet? Religious scholars of both sexes are paying careful attention to such questions, because the answers could lead to decisions that limit or increase women's rights in synagogues, churches, and mosques today.

Within Christianity, church officials debate the role of women as priests or pastors. While mainstream denominations such as the Presbyterians, Episcopalians, and Methodists have women bishops, two of the largest U.S. denominations, the Mormons and Southern Baptists, forbid women from holding church offices. Christian scholars disagree

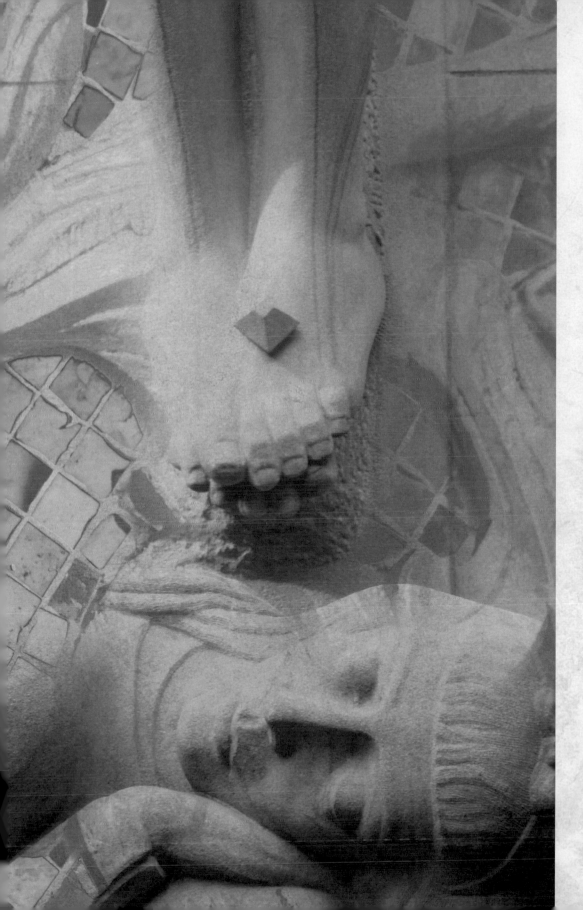

"Radical feminists and others have denigrated the traditional roles of women as partner, wife and mother in their effort to promote women as individuals whose fulfillment is to be found almost exclusively in the workplace. Most women are trying to find a balance between responsibilities to family and children and using their gifts in the workplace. They will be happier if they have a conscious appreciation of their irreplaceable role as feminine persons with a special gift for affirming the life of other persons."

—*from a Catholic writer and former nun, on Catholic Online*

among themselves in their understanding of the Bible. Some point to passages that appear to limit women's authority in churches, yet others point to verses that seem to encourage female leadership. Some of the largest *evangelical* churches in North America, including the 20,000-member Willow Creek Church, encourage women to seek leadership, and evangelical schools such as Fuller Theological Seminary support women in ministry.

For many people of faith, scripture determines what is wrong or right in the sight of God. In the next chapter, we take a whirlwind tour through time to learn what the Bible says about women's roles in society, in religion, and in the home.

DAUGHTERS OF EVE
Women in Bible Times

The city of Abel was under attack. Troops surrounded the city walls, like angry bees swarming over a hive. Battering rams smashed away at the foundations of the ramparts, and a horde of enraged warriors prepared to rush in.

In the midst of his troops, King David's general Joab directed the siege. For weeks, his army had pursued Sheba, a rebel against the king. When Joab's army approached the walls of Abel, alarmed citizens shut the massive gates. Joab was more used to killing than negotiating, so he promptly gave orders to attack.

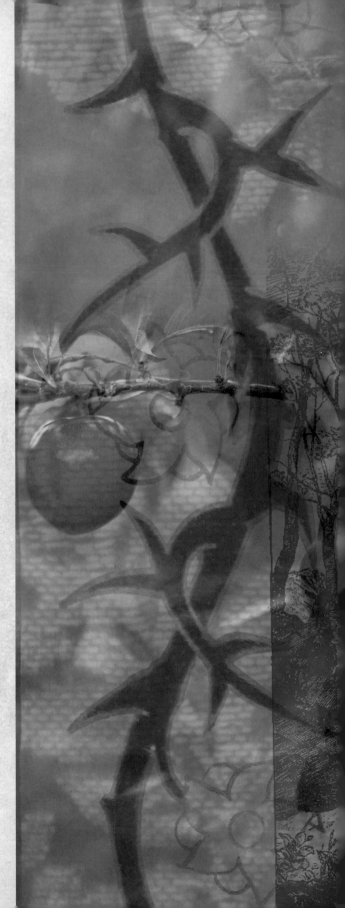

Over the din of shouts and clanking armor, a woman's voice rang out. "Listen to me, Joab. Come over here so I can talk to you." The sounds of attack grew suddenly quiet. Who would have the courage to speak to the king's commander like that? Joab knew it was common for women to hold substantial power in the cities of Judah, serving as "wise women" and guiding the decisions of the citizens; he assumed this must be such a person.

As he approached the wall, the woman called out again, her voice strong and confident. "Are you Joab?"

"I am," the general replied.

She said, "Listen carefully to your servant."

"I'm listening," Joab barked back.

The woman called down, "I am one who is peace loving and faithful in Israel. But you are destroying a loyal city. Why do you want to destroy what belongs to the people?"

Joab replied, "Believe me, I don't want to destroy your city! All I want is a man named Sheba, who has revolted against King David. If you hand him over to me, we will leave the city in peace."

There was a moment's pause as the general and his troops awaited her decision.

"All right," she replied. "We will throw his head over the wall to you."

The Bible concludes this historical account by saying, "Then the woman went to the people with her wise advice, and they cut off Sheba's head and threw it out to Joab. So he blew the trumpet and called his troops back from the attack, and they all returned to their homes" (2 Samuel 20:22, New Living Translation [NLT]).

Modern readers sometimes assume women in Bible times were timid, second-class citizens doing whatever males told them. It is true that men dominated women in the ancient Near East, and the Bible records this historical reality, but readers of the ancient text will find a surpris-

GLOSSARY

Gnosticism: The thought and practice of various cults of late pre-Christian and early Christian centuries that was distinguished by the conviction that concrete, tangible reality is evil and that spiritual freedom comes from secret and mysterious practices.

prophesy: To teach others religious ideas based on divine inspiration.

rabbis: Jewish teachers.

Western: Found in or typical of countries whose culture and society are influenced by traditions rooted in Greek and Roman culture and Christianity, especially countries in Europe and North and South America.

ing number of strong and independent women. While some scholars believe the Bible authors were sexist, others see them as supporting women's equality.

CREATED EQUAL

Genesis 1:27 says, "God created people in his own image; God patterned them after himself; male and female he created them" (NLT). Shortly afterward, God told both the man and the woman to "be masters" over

"You are each an Eve. . . . The sentence of God on this sex of yours lives on even in our times and so it is necessary that the guilt should live on, also. You are the one who opened the door to the devil."

—Tertullian, *famous second-century preacher, from a sermon addressing Christian women*

the earth (verse 28). Thus, in the beginning, there is no difference between the rights of the man or the woman, both rule over the earth. Furthermore, God has both male and female qualities, since both sexes express God's "image."

In Genesis 2:18, God said, "It is not good for the man to be alone. I will make him a companion who will help him." To some people, the word "help" implies the woman is a servant, or assistant, as Helen Andelin put it, "a smiling, tender little domestic goddess." Yet the English word "help" can also mean partner, ally, or coworker, and that is closer to the meaning of the Hebrew word used in this verse. In the Old Testament, the word "helper" often describes what God does. Even five centuries ago, when sexism was rampant, John Calvin said Moses (the author of Genesis) "intended to note some equality" between the sexes.

BLAME IT ON THE WOMAN

Genesis chapter 3 describes the tragedy of humanity's fall from perfect union with God. God created a wonderful planet and gave the man and woman just one instruction—avoid eating the forbidden fruit of Good and Evil. For centuries, male preachers blamed the first woman (and women in general) for bringing evil into the world. Based on such thinking, men taught that women are more willing to give in to temptation, and more prone to evil.

DATING SYSTEMS & THEIR MEANING

You might be accustomed to seeing dates expressed with the abbreviations BC or AD, as in the year 1000 BC or the year AD 1900. For centuries, this dating system has been the most common in the Western world. However, since BC and AD are based on Christianity (BC stands for Before Christ and AD stands for *anno Domini*, Latin for "in the year of our Lord"), many people now prefer abbreviations that people from all religions can be comfortable using. The abbreviations BCE (meaning Before Common Era) and CE (meaning Common Era) mark time in the same way as BC and AD (for example, 1000 BC is the same year as 1000 BCE, and AD 1900 is the same year as 1900 CE), but BCE and CE do not have the same religious overtones as BC and AD.

This tendency to blame women for all the world's ills had more to do with prejudice than with careful Bible study, as the Bible appears to blame both partners for the beginning of sin. Genesis 3:6 says Adam "was with her" when Eve ate the forbidden fruit. Perhaps that is why the Apostle Paul, in Roman's 5:12, speaks of the first sin as "Adam's sin" rather than that of Eve.

RELIGION & MODERN CULTURE

THE (FEMALE) DEVIL MADE ME DO IT

Portraying events in the Garden of Eden, some artists of the Middle Ages went beyond blaming the woman (Eve) for humanity's woes. They made the serpent a woman as well! For example, Michelangelo, in his famous Sistine Chapel painting, clearly shows a snake wrapped around the forbidden tree, with a woman's exposed breast, face, and long hair. The idea of a female devil resurfaced more recently in the movie *Bedazzled*, in which Elizabeth Hurley portrayed the charming prince—make that princess—of darkness.

According to the biblical account, after Adam and Eve ate the forbidden fruit, the whole world changed as suffering and human conflict entered the world. God predicted one form of sin, sexism, saying to Eve, "your husband, he will be your master" (Genesis 3:16, NLT). Many Bible scholars say that while this describes the way things happen in the world, it does not express what God desired when creating men and women. It is the consequence of human wrongdoing.

ISRAEL'S JOAN OF ARC

In 1100 BCE, the Israelites were weary from war. The book of Judges, chapter 4 says, "Deborah, the wife of Lappidoth, was a prophet who became a judge in Israel." The word "judge" does not refer to someone like Judge Judy; Deborah was not banging a gavel in the courtroom. The judges of ancient Israel were like kings: the nation did as they commanded. As the chapter continues, Deborah summons Barak, a commander in Israel's army, and orders him to, "Assemble ten thousand warriors." Barak replies, "I will go, but only if you go with me." Deborah agrees and tells Barak "the Lord's victory . . . will be at the hands of a woman." It is only recently that laws have allowed women to serve as leaders in the U.S. military, and there has not been a female U.S. president to date, yet three thousand years ago, a woman led the nation of Israel.

GHASTLY ABUSES

Though the book of Judges records how Deborah led Israel, that same book includes cases of horrible brutality against women. In chapter 11, a judge named Jephthah offers his teenage daughter as a human sacrifice. In chapter 19, "wicked men" in the city of Gibeah rape and kill an unnamed woman. In the final chapter of Judges, a tribe of men attack the women of Shiloh in the middle of a sacred dance, taking them by force to be wives. The Bible writers recorded but did not approve of such sins against women.

AN ANCIENT CAREER WOMAN

Five hundred years after Deborah's time, the author of Proverbs described "a wife of noble character." In the twenty-first century, many women still struggle to balance their roles as mothers, wives, and

"Perhaps it is no wonder that the women were first at the Cradle and last at the Cross. They had never known a man like this Man—there has never been such another. A prophet and teacher who never nagged at them, never flattered or coaxed or patronized; who never made arch jokes about them . . . who took their questions and arguments seriously."

—Dorothy Sayers, famous British author of the last century

business professionals, yet this woman of around 600 BCE knew how to handle both her family and business successfully. Proverbs 31 tells how this woman began her own business: "She goes out to inspect a field and buys it; with her earnings she plants a vineyard" (Proverbs 31:16, NLT). In addition to her vineyard, the woman also manufactures clothing: "She makes belted linen garments and sashes to sell to the merchants" (verse 24). Along with running two businesses, she manages her children and gives charity to the poor. For some modern women, the "wife of noble character" is a discouraging role model; they wonder how anyone can compare with a woman like that. Bible scholars point out that she may be imaginary—an ideal picture of womanhood—but she proves people in Old Testament times expected women to do well in business as well as family roles; they were more liberated than most North American women were until the 1960s.

MY BIG FAT GREEK PREJUDICE

The ancient Greeks get credit for inventing many of the good things in *Western* civilization—art, philosophy, the Olympics, and democracy. However, they did not have a good record regarding women's rights. Some viewers were surprised that the recent movie *Alexander* portrayed Alexander the Great in a homosexual relationship—but ancient Greek men had homosexual lovers because they believed women were not smart enough to be romantic partners, and women could not vote or participate in public discussions.

In 332 BCE, Alexander the Great conquered the Holy Land, and Greek thinking controlled Jewish life for the next three centuries. During this time, the Jewish religion adopted the sexist views of their Greek conquerors. Rabbi Eliezer said, "Let the words of the Torah be burnt rather than give them to a woman!" The Jewish historian Josephus, who lived at the same time as Jesus of Nazareth, wrote, "The woman is inferior to the man in every way." These were common attitudes at the time when Jesus, the son of Mary, came into the world.

THE RADICAL RABBI

Jesus of Nazareth was unique for his time in the way he respected women. Other religious teachers avoided "fallen" women, refusing even to enter a street if a prostitute were walking on it. Jesus honored the faith of an "immoral" woman who anointed him with oil (Luke, chapter 7). Other *rabbis* forbade teaching religion to women, yet Jesus taught Mary and Martha in their home (Luke 10:39). Courts did not allow women to give legal testimony since they regarded them as unreliable, yet Jesus commanded women to spread the good news of his resurrection (Luke 24).

34

Modern scholars agree that Jesus's treatment of women was extraordinary. Marcus Borg says, "One of the most remarkable features of Jesus' ministry was his relationship to women. Challenging the conventional wisdom of his time, it continues to challenge the conventional wisdom of much of the church." Likewise, Bible scholar Mary Evans writes, "To Jesus, the intrinsic value of women as persons is just as great as that of men, an idea found nowhere in, and in some ways alien to, the Jewish thought of the time." In the same vein, author Philip Yancey comments, "For women and other oppressed people, Jesus turned upside down the accepted wisdom of his day."

While modern scholars agree Jesus was unique among ancient religious leaders in his respect for women, some feel Christianity is, nonetheless, sexist. Jesus was the son of God, and he appointed twelve male apostles, hence, salvation still comes to the world through men. Others wonder if centuries of male authors did not erase or diminish women's presence from Jesus's actual story. Mary Magdalene may not have been Jesus's wife—but she was certainly one of his disciples.

THE APOSTLE PAUL—WOMAN HATER OR LIBERATOR?

Modern scholars agree Jesus was a true friend to women, but they are not so certain about Paul of Tarsus, who wrote most of the New Testament. Various writers have termed Paul "sexist" and a "woman hater." On the other hand, historian Thomas Cahill claims, "Women were as free to speak, to evangelize, and to administer in the Pauline churches as was any man." How can Bible readers say such different things about the Apostle Paul?

Paul mentions women who held important roles in the first Christian churches, such as Phoebe, described in Romans, 16:1. The New American Bible translation says Phoebe is a "minister," and the New Living Bible says "deacon." Shortly after New Testament times, Bishop

Ignatius said Christians should "respect the deacons as the command-ments of God," so it seems Phoebe was an important person in the early church. The same chapter, verse 7, mentions Junia who is "prominent among the apostles." Junia is a female name, but in some Bibles, trans-lators changed Junia into Junias, which is a man's name, because they did not believe an apostle could be a woman. In ancient Roman culture, women served as lawyers, politicians, and doctors, but the Greek cities denied women equal rights.

Paul recognized how important women were in the church, and he penned two great statements regarding women's equality. In Galatians 3:28 he wrote, "There is no longer Jew or Gentile, slave or free, *male or female*, for you are all Christians—you are one in Christ Jesus" (NLT). Ancient Romans assumed slaves and women were born inferior, so this was a radical statement. Likewise, in 1 Corinthians 7:4 he wrote: "the husband does not rule over his own body, but the wife does" (Revised Standard Version). This saying must have hit the Roman world like a bombshell, because everyone assumed husbands owned their wives' bodies. No one had ever dared to suggest the wife had ownership of her husband.

DID THE APOSTLE PAUL RESTRICT WOMEN'S RIGHTS?

If his letters contain such liberating statements as those above, why do some people call Paul "sexist"? This charge comes from two other verses allegedly from the apostle's pen. One is 1 Corinthians 14:34:

> Women should be silent during the church meetings. It is not proper for them to speak. . . . If they have any questions let them ask their husbands at home, for it is improper for women to speak in church meetings. (NLT)

There is a strange thing about this verse; it contradicts what Paul says in chapter 11 of the same book, where he mentions women

"praying and prophesying" in church. How could Paul expect women to pray and *prophesy* if he did not allow them to speak? Some Bible scholars believe a later scribe added these verses to the Apostle Paul's letter. Others suggest that women, who had been denied any schooling in this Greek city, were asking questions aloud in the middle of worship services and were disrupting worship for everyone else, thus Paul instructed them to stay quiet so other people could learn. Sometimes people forget that when Paul was writing his letters, he was directing his thoughts toward a particular community experiencing a specific situation; he did not know his words would be read and taken to heart by centuries of Christians.

"If she have the necessary gifts, and feels herself called by the Spirit to preach, there is not a single word in the whole book of God to restrain her, but many, very many, to urge her and encourage her."

—*Catherine Booth, cofounder of the Salvation Army*

The other "sexist" verse attributed to Paul is 1 Timothy 2:12: "I do not let women teach men or have authority over them" (NLT). Because of this one verse, for centuries churches have denied women the right to preach. Professor Catherine Clark Kroeger, an expert on classical studies teaching at Gordon Conwell Theological Seminary, has done some intriguing study on this verse. She notes that the word translated "have authority" is an unusual Greek word that would be better rendered "seize or take over authority." Kroeger also points out that Paul was writing to a church troubled by a form of Christianity called **Gnosticism**. The Gnostics appealed especially to women, and Gnostic teachers sometimes tried to take over churches. Kroeger suggests Paul meant to forbid Gnostic women from taking over the Ephesian church; he would have no problem with women pastors who taught his form of Christianity. Yet other scholars, differing with Kroeger, argue that Paul intended to limit church authority to men for all churches and all times.

Was Paul a supporter of women's rights, or did he go along with the sexism of the ancient world? Should modern Christians understand his letters as pertaining only to history, or would he say the same things today? Bible scholars continue to debate these important questions.

Meanwhile, of all the women in the Bible, Jesus's mother Mary is most famous. Over the centuries, Mary has become far more than a biblical figure—she has taken on new identities as the Queen of Heaven, Our Lady of Peace, and even the Mother of God.

Chapter 3

THE MOTHER OF GOD

Philip Koufos, pastor of Chicago's St. Nicholas Albanian Orthodox Church, was busy lighting candles for a special service on December 6, 1986, when he noticed moisture on an ***icon*** of the Virgin Mary. At first, he thought someone had carelessly spilled water, but then he looked closer and saw that tears were pouring from the Virgin's eyes. He summoned two church members, who saw the same thing. The painting wept for the next seven months, then less frequently until 1994, when it began weeping regularly again. Albanian refugees in the congregation thought Mary shed tears because of the way the government mistreated Christians in their homeland. In the past two decades, more than two million people have visited St. Nicholas Church to see the weeping icon.

In the history of Christianity, the Virgin Mary has received more attention than any figure other than Jesus himself. She is the subject of innumerable songs, poems, prayers, altars, statues, chapels, churches, and reported appearances. She has gained titles—Mother of God, Queen of Heaven, and Lady of Sorrows. She is also part of popular culture—tattooed on biceps, painted on bakery windows, and molded as tiny plastic figures adorning car dashboards.

Two thousand years after she lived, Mary of Nazareth has become much more than a historical figure: she is one of history's most important myths. A Roman Catholic Web site offers the following definition of myth:

> An imaginative story using symbols and colorful images to help us understand a truth either too complicated or too difficult to express in words. Unfortunately, most modern readers consider *myth* to be equivalent to *fairy tale*—a good story perhaps, but without truth. This understanding of myth, however, is very different from what the sacred writer and biblical scholar would intend. A myth is a human way of exploring and dealing with a mysterious truth.

Many Christians claim their beliefs are both powerful myths *and* historical realities.

MARY & SCRIPTURE

The Gospel accounts of Mary begin with the **annunciation** that she has become miraculously pregnant. In Luke's gospel, the angel Gabriel appears to the Virgin, who was probably a teenager at the time, engaged but not married to Joseph. The angel tells her, "God has decided to bless

GLOSSARY

annunciation: Announcement.

icon: A holy picture used as a focus for prayer and worship.

idolatry: Worshipping something or someone other than God.

Marian: Pertaining to Mary, mother of Jesus.

you! You will become pregnant and have a son, and you are to name him Jesus" (Luke 1:31, NLT). In reply, "Mary asked the angel, 'But how can I have a baby? I am a virgin'" (1:34). Like most Jewish girls of her time, she was saving sex for marriage, so this pregnancy was confusing to say the least. The angel replied, "The Holy Spirit will come upon you, and the power of the Most High will overshadow you. So the baby born to you will be holy, and he will be called the Son of God" (1:35).

Skeptics point out that Greek and Roman legends also describe sexual encounters between the gods and mortals. Could such legends have inspired the nativity stories in the Gospels? Bible-believing scholars reply that the Jews had no such legends, and in fact, they disdained Greco-Roman mythology, so why should they of all people imitate Pagan fables?

Shortly after she became pregnant, Mary headed out of town, escaping the embarrassment and pressure of facing those who knew her, as many young pregnant women have done throughout history. According

to the Gospel account, Mary went to stay with her cousin Elizabeth; while she was there, she composed a song known in Latin as the "Magnificat." Evangelical Bible scholar Scott McKnight says this song contains "virtually every theme in Jesus' teaching and ministry. . . . I think she sang him [baby Jesus] to sleep with these kinds of songs and had a profound influence on him."

Luke records that Mary and Joseph took baby Jesus to Jerusalem for dedication, as some Christians take their babies to church for christening today. At the Jerusalem temple, a prophet named Simeon declared, "I have seen the Savior," but he warned the new mother, "a sword will pierce your soul," a prediction of Mary's agony while watching her son's death on the cross decades later.

You would think raising God's son would be easy—but the Bible doesn't say so. When he was twelve, Mary and Joseph traveled with Jesus to Jerusalem, where he left them in the big city. They spent three days looking for him, finally finding him in the temple, holding deep spiritual discussions with the priests. "Son!' His mother said to him. "Why have you done this to us? Your father and I have been frantic, searching for you everywhere" (Luke 2:48, NLT). Jesus replied, "You should have known that I would be in my father's house" (2:49).

Joseph disappears from Bible history after this incident, and scholars assume he died while Jesus was young. Mary continued to follow her son's career; according to the Gospel of John, she influenced Jesus to perform his first miracle—turning 180 gallons of water into wine for a wedding party. She followed her son faithfully, even when most of the disciples abandoned him at the cross. John recounts how, struggling for breath and bleeding internally, "Jesus saw his mother standing . . . beside the disciple he loved, and he said to her, 'Woman, he is your son.' And he said to this disciple, 'She is your mother.' And from then on this disciple took her into his home" (John 19:26–27, NLT). Even in his suffering, Jesus was concerned for his mother.

45

"Our Christian tradition has many beautiful and exalting teachings about Mary the Mother of Jesus whom we have come to recognize as the Mother of God."

—Virgilio Elizondo, Professor of Religion at Notre Dame

According to Catholic interpreters, Mary appears in the last book of the Bible as "a woman clothed with the sun, with the moon beneath her feet, and a crown of twelve stars on her head" (Revelation 12:1). Then Jesus's mother disappears from the Bible. However, innumerable traditions about Mary took on a life of their own over the following centuries.

THE MARY OF CATHOLIC DOGMA

Over the centuries, Catholic authorities have established four **Marian** Doctrines—official Church beliefs about the Virgin. The first is her role as Mother of God. In 431 CE, bishops of the Catholic Church met at the city of Ephesus, where they publicly declared Mary to be "Mother of God." The citizens of the city were so happy they took all two hundred bishops on their shoulders and marched them around in a parade. They based the title Mother of God on Luke 1:43, where Elizabeth declares Mary to be "the mother of my Lord."

A century later, the Church established the second Marian Doctrine, her perpetual virginity, stating Mary never had sex before, during, or after her pregnancy. At this time in Church history, male theologians connected sexual intercourse with sin and forbade priests from marrying. Mary's perpetual virginity both reflected and reinforced these beliefs.

It took more than a thousand years for the Catholic Church to declare a third Marian Doctrine, the Immaculate Conception. The Immaculate Conception is based on the Angel's declaration, "Hail Mary, full of Grace" (Luke 1:28) and states that the Virgin was utterly holy—without any sin at all—from the moment she was conceived and throughout her entire life.

The Catholic Church did not declare the last of the Marian Doctrines until the twentieth century, that being the assumption of Mary into heaven. According to this doctrine, after Mary died, she immediately rose to life and went up to heaven, just as her son had done, where she sits at his right hand as Queen Mother.

A MOTHER'S LOVE

Since the book of Hebrews declares Jesus to be "in every respect like us, his brothers and sisters" (Hebrews 2:17), many Christians believe Jesus's mother is their mother as well. The Vatican II Council of the Catholic Church declared, "The Mother of God . . . is mother of Christ and mother of men, particularly of the faithful." Mothers care for their children no matter what bad things the children have done; likewise believers trust that Mother Mary will be available to help them, whatever their sins.

A popular medieval legend shows how far Mary's mercy would go: A cannibal ate seventy-eight people, including his own family members. When he died the demons of hell set out to claim his soul, but the Virgin Mary took the man from them. Mary escorted the cannibal's soul to her Son, and explained to Jesus that this man had once given a beggar a cup of water, "for Mary's sake." Jesus weighed the man's deeds. On one side of a scale, he placed a cup of water given for Mary's sake, and on the other side of the scale, he placed the seventy-eight souls of the cannibal's victims. The cup of water outweighed the seventy-eight souls, and

MARY OF THE AMERICAS

On December of 1531, on a little hill near Mexico City, Mary appeared as Our Lady of Guadalupe (*Nuestra Señora de Guadalupe*) to an Indian, Juan Diego, who was en route to Mexico City. She was dark skinned like Juan Diego and spoke to him in Nahuatl, the Aztec language. As proof of this miraculous appearance, she gave Juan Diego a sign, her image miraculously painted on his cape. Today, the cape hangs in a shrine in Mexico City, where thousands of pilgrims come annually to give honor to Guadalupe. Not only popular in Mexico but throughout the entire hemisphere, the Catholic Church has declared her to be "Protectress of the Americas."

bal's victims. The cup of water outweighed the seventy-eight souls, and the cannibal was saved! No wonder many Catholics repeat the rosary prayer that ends with an appeal to Mary, "Pray for us sinners, now and at the hour of our death."

Many Catholics rely on Mother Mary not only for forgiveness, but also for physical needs. Visitors leave crutches and plaques at places like Lourdes, France, and Marpingen, Germany, as signs that Mary has healed them. In Spain and Central America, there are elaborate processions during Holy Week in which floats with representations of Mary are more elaborate than those that portray her son. It is Mary who receives the "ohs" and "ahs" from those admiring the procession.

"In her suffering Mary becomes the universal mother because there is no parent who cannot identify with her. She, like all parents, is the mother who suffers in the deepest recesses of her being the fate of her children. Yet every parent can equally gain strength from her."

—*Virgilio Elizondo*

OUR LADY OF SORROWS

Mothers always love their children even when those children go astray or get hurt, and because of that, mothers often cry a lot. Many people believe Mary also cries a lot, hence one of her names—Our Lady of Sorrows.

In 2004, Catholic filmmaker Mel Gibson presented the world with *The Passion of the Christ*. It was a surprise hit, selling $84 million in tickets the first week. Protestants responded enthusiastically to the film, especially its depiction of Jesus's mother. Catholics have a tradition of Mary's suffering, "the seven maternal sorrows," but most Protestants had not considered how terrible she must have felt when her son was tortured and killed. *The Passion of the Christ* introduced a wide audience to Our Lady of Sorrows.

Catholics who report miraculous appearances of Mary often state that she is crying. In 1846, when two young shepherds at La Salette, France, spied a young woman weeping, they assumed her family had abused her, as that was their own experience. They were amazed when she told them she was the Virgin Mary and faded from their sight.

As Michael Durham says in his book *Miracles of Mary*, "By crying, some believe, she establishes a rapport with those who have led hard and discouraging lives." The March 21, 2005, issue of *Time* magazine re-

MARY APPEARS TO BOTH CHRISTIANS & MUSLIMS IN EGYPT

Muslims revere Mary, whom the Holy Qur'an exalts in more than a dozen verses (see especially Surah 3 Section 5). Between 1968 and 1971, Mary allegedly appeared repeatedly at night, illuminated atop a church in Zeitoun, Egypt. Large crowds observed her, the majority of whom were Muslim. Egyptian police investigated, hoping to explain the sightings as hoaxes, but they had to admit their failure to explain the events. One witness to the appearance was Egyptian president Abdul Nasser. According to a Coptic priest serving the church, Mary's appearances were good for the country because, "It makes some unity between Christians and Muslims."

counts the story of a Baptist woman who found surprising comfort from the Virgin. When a friend died in a plane crash, this woman retreated to a Catholic convent. She was up one night, "sobbing and praying and asking why" and found herself in front of a statue of Mary, portrayed with outstretched arms and a sympathetic face. "I realized that she knew what it was like to see her son die on the Cross, to bear that sorrow and grief. I felt she was giving me a window into the compassion God had for me in my own experience." Now a chaplain, this Baptist has an office filled with images of Mary.

53

PROTESTANTS & MARY

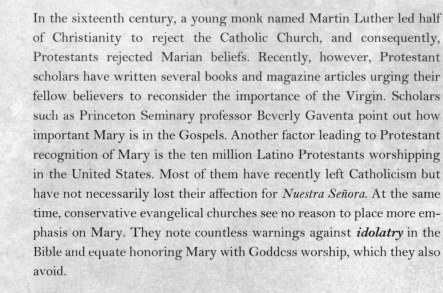

In the sixteenth century, a young monk named Martin Luther led half of Christianity to reject the Catholic Church, and consequently, Protestants rejected Marian beliefs. Recently, however, Protestant scholars have written several books and magazine articles urging their fellow believers to reconsider the importance of the Virgin. Scholars such as Princeton Seminary professor Beverly Gaventa point out how important Mary is in the Gospels. Another factor leading to Protestant recognition of Mary is the ten million Latino Protestants worshipping in the United States. Most of them have recently left Catholicism but have not necessarily lost their affection for *Nuestra Señora*. At the same time, conservative evangelical churches see no reason to place more emphasis on Mary. They note countless warnings against **idolatry** in the Bible and equate honoring Mary with Goddess worship, which they also avoid.

IS MARY A GOOD OR BAD ROLE MODEL FOR MODERN WOMEN?

Catholic and Protestant women debate Mary's relevance in the twenty-first century. Some believe Mary is a good model for female worshippers. Timothy Matovina writes in the Catholic weekly magazine *America* about the influence of Nuestra Señora in San Fernando Cathedral in San Antonio, Texas. According to Matovina, faith in the Virgin has enabled women at the cathedral to believe they have a greater role in the home and in community activism, politics, and community affairs. Esther, a member of the parish, says, "Guadalupe gives you [women] dignity to go places you haven't been before."

Catholics point out that Mary has real power as the Queen of Heaven. In the Old Testament, the Queen Mother sat at the right side of Israel's king and served as chief counselor to the monarch. Likewise, Mary sits at the side of her Son as he reigns in glory, powerful over the universe. She is wise, noble, and exalted—isn't that a positive female role model?

On the other hand, some women see the Virgin's influence as negative, saying her virginity adds to the stereotype that sex is evil. Marina Warner, a former Catholic and author of *Alone of All Her Sex: the Myth and the Cult of the Virgin Mary*, believes Mary is a destructive role model. Catholics tell young women to imitate the Virgin, but that is impossible because the roles of mother and virgin conflict. According to Warner, the mixed messages of "avoid sex as evil" and "strive to be a mother with many children" create feelings of confusion and guilt in Catholic women. Furthermore, Mary submissively goes along with the program set by male figures around her (God, the Angel, and Joseph), so for critics, the Virgin Mary is a myth designed to encourage women's submission to men.

Marina Warner and other critics say belief in Mary is likely to fade away in the coming decades, as a myth no longer meaningful to modern worshippers. Other religious scholars disagree, however, since interest in Mary is increasing throughout churches in the first years of the twenty-first century. Mary has never been more popular.

MARY AS THE FEMININE DEITY

For the past five centuries, Protestants have charged that Catholic and Orthodox Christians confuse Mary's role with that of God's. Officially, both churches have strongly avoided doing so. They emphasize that Christians should not worship Mary but merely honor her. Furthermore, believers are not to pray *to* Mary but pray *through her*,

asking her to intercede with her Son. Catholic religion professor Scott Hahn points out that Mary is a coworker with God, just as the Bible says that all Christians are God's coworkers.

Even though Christian churches carefully distance the Virgin Mary from God, popular beliefs have sometimes raised her to divine status. In the book *La Diosa de las Americas (the Goddess of the Americas)*, Jeanette Rodriguez, associate professor of religion at Seattle University, contributes a chapter titled "Guadalupe: The Feminine Face of God." Rodriguez says that European conquerors presented God to Native people as overwhelming, powerful, and angry—like the conquistadors themselves. The Virgin Mary, however, showed Native people God's mercy and loving kindness. Thus, Rodriguez suggests Latin Americans learned about God's love by looking to the Virgin.

Historians point out connections between the worship of Mary and Goddess worship. Visions of Mary and reported healings often occur at wells, places previously associated with "maidens of the well" or water goddesses. The Virgin of Guadalupe appeared above the ancient shrine of an Aztec goddess, and Mexicans still pray to Mary by the name of that goddess, Tonantzin. The "Black Madonna," revered in more than four hundred locations throughout France, was preceded by the mother goddess Black Artemis in the same region. These ideas do not disturb Catholic thinkers: perhaps, they say, God was preparing Pagans for the day when God's Mother appeared.

Skeptics sometimes ask why people of faith spend so much time studying and debating their beliefs. Why should invisible things matter? Sociologists, however, point out that religious beliefs matter greatly because they powerfully influence behaviors. They have also affected women's rights in church, family, and society.

Chapter 4

A WOMAN'S PLACE IN CHURCH, SYNAGOGUE, & MOSQUE

RELIGION & MODERN CULTURE

Anne Graham Lotz is the daughter of world famous evangelist Billy Graham and his wife Ruth Bell Graham. As a young woman, Anne learned she had a gift for teaching the Bible, and she received many invitations to speak at Christian gatherings. However, even with her talent and family heritage, Anne has faced challenges as a woman in **conservative** Protestant churches. One time the organizers of a pastors' conference asked her to speak, but many of the attending pastors were opposed to women preaching. Therefore, dozens of pastors stood up and turned their backs to her when she spoke. Anne Graham Lotz has addressed thousands of pastors and missionaries, yet she has never served as pastor in a church because she comes from the Southern Baptist tradition that denies women the authority to preach.

Historians debate the extent of women's leadership in the very beginning of the Christian church, but there is general agreement that women held greater authority in the first century than they did afterward. Karen Jo Torjesen, dean at the Claremont School of Religion and an expert on women in ancient Christianity, notes in her book *When Women Were Priests,* that an ancient Roman inscription concerning "Theodora Episcopa" means "Bishop Theodora"—a woman bishop of the early Christian church.

In the year 325, the Catholic Church forbade women from the priesthood. Around this time, the Church declared that sin was transmitted by sexual intercourse, and they praised monks and nuns for their avoidance of sex and marriage. This negative view of sex increased sexism in Christian churches and Western society. Thomas Aquinas, the most famous medieval theologian, preached, "The woman is subject to the man, on account of the weakness of her nature, both of mind and of body. Children ought to love their father more than their mother." Martin Luther, the father of Protestant Christianity, likewise said, "Men have broad shoulders and narrow hips, and accordingly they possess intelligence. Women have narrow shoulders and broad hips . . . to sit upon, keep house and bear children."

Despite such prejudice, women made some great accomplishments during the Middle Ages. Traditions say that in the late 400s, Brigid of Ireland served as bishop. Several centuries later, Hilda of Whitby ruled a religious community of both men and women, where she trained five future bishops and kings sought her advice. In the twelfth century, a woman, Hildegard of Bingen, wrote the first Christian drama, and the first autobiography in the English language was written by a woman, Margery Kempe, in the early 1400s.

Women were influential in evangelical churches of the nineteenth and twentieth centuries. In England in the 1800s, a husband-and-wife

GLOSSARY

chattel: An item of personal property that is not land and not intangible.

conservative: Resistant to new ideas and change.

excommunicated: Officially removed from fellowship with or membership in a group or organization.

liberal: Open to new ideas and change.

team, William and Catherine Booth, who encouraged women to preach and evangelize, founded the Salvation Army. During the same years in the United States, Methodist evangelist Phoebe Palmer spoke to over 100,000 people and fueled a revival that brought almost a million people into Christian churches. In the first part of the twentieth century, Aimee Semple McPherson was the United States' most popular preacher. She ordered construction of Angelus Temple, one of the largest churches of the time, was the first woman with a nationally broadcast radio show, and established 410 churches with 29,000 members. In the mid-twentieth century, Henrietta Mears of Hollywood Presbyterian Church taught Sunday School, influencing Billy Graham and various Hollywood celebrities. She also cofounded Gospel Light Publications, one of the first publishers in the Christian-education field.

"If your Bible is an argument for the degradation of woman, and the abuse by whipping of little children, I advise you to put it away, and use your common sense instead."

—*Lucy Colman, abolitionist, 1887*

WOMEN'S ROLES IN NORTH AMERICAN CHRISTIANITY TODAY

The Catholic Church forbids women from serving as priests; many Catholic women in the United States and Canada find themselves at odds with this teaching. A recent Canadian survey found that two out of three Catholics say their church's view of sex roles is "outdated"; a 2002 survey in the United States found similar results. Officials in Rome, however, seem little concerned about demands by North American women for greater roles. In 1993, Pope John Paul II issued a document titled "On Priestly Ordination" that contained the strongest statement in the history of the Church opposing female priests.

Though barred from the priesthood, women have found ways to provide leadership in Catholic congregations. There are not enough priests in North America to serve all the churches, so to make up for this shortage, many congregations hire female "pastoral administrators," who serve under the local priest to provide counseling, hospital visitation, and practical assistance to congregation members. They can give Bible lessons and say prayers during services. Some even lead worship services using bread and wine that has earlier been blessed by the priest. In the United States, approximately 16,000 women are serving as Catholic pastoral administrators. Charles Morris, author of the book *American Catholic*, asked a woman in a Houston Catholic church what she thought about women priests, who replied, "We already run the church." Many members of Catholic parishes would agree.

HALLELUJAH GALS

In 1880, when the Salvation Army sent their first team of evangelists from Great Britain to America, all seven missionaries were women, known as "the Hallelujah Gals." They preached in the streets, near saloons, and in the roughest parts of squalid cities where hostile crowds greeted them with jeering, threats, thrown food, and sometimes violence. Despite these rough conditions, they established ten separate churches in three months, conducting more than 200 services each week. Their amazing success caused Salvation Army cofounder William Booth to exclaim, "My best men are women."

Abortion is a controversial topic among North Americans in general, and U.S. and Canadian Catholics often disagree with the official teachings of the Church on this matter. Surveys taken in 1998 and 2002 show a majority of U.S. Catholics favor legalized abortion. Another survey found division among Canadians, who are 70 percent Catholic, regarding abortion. The majority of Canadians believe abortion should be legal in some cases, differing with Catholic teaching that abortion should be illegal under all circumstances.

RELIGION & MODERN CULTURE

MON TUE WED
LUN MAR MER

"It doesn't matter if we agree with our husbands or not. It doesn't matter if we want to do what they ask of us. If it isn't out of line with the Word of God, we shouldn't have a problem submitting ourselves to our husbands and doing as they ask. . . . It's not a question . . . if the man should be the head of the household. He is. Period. The Lord appointed man the responsibility of being the head of the household."

—*from "a Christian wife and mother" posted on her personal Web site*

If abortion causes disagreement between some Catholic women and the Church, the issue of birth control causes even greater disagreement with Church teaching. In 1968, the Church issued a statement titled "Humanae Vitae," which made it clear that artificial methods of birth control (including the pill, diaphragm, and condom) are forbidden for Catholics. Pope John Paul II declared such birth control to be "evil." Despite such strong condemnation from the Church, 96 percent of U.S. Catholic couples in a recent survey admitted their use of contraceptives.

Thomas Fox, in his book *Sexuality and Catholicism*, notes one reason for the difference between official Church teaching and the opinions of North American Catholic women. "It is women who are dominated by men, women who become pregnant, women who carry the unborn, and women who give birth," but only men make authoritative decisions for the Catholic Church.

Unlike the Roman Catholic Church, evangelicals lack unified religious leadership; hence, evangelicals today hold differing views on women's roles in churches and in families. Some believe men should be in leadership over women, both in homes and in churches, yet other evangelicals insist either women or men can exercise leadership. Some evangelical women say they like their husbands to lead the family, but others feel demeaned by such practice. The largest U.S. Protestant denomination, the Southern Baptist Convention, officially stated in 2000 that, "While both men and women are gifted for service in the church, the office of pastor is limited to men." On the other hand, America's largest church, Willow Creek, encourages women to serve along with men as pastors, as do many other evangelical churches. Mainstream Protestant churches (Methodist, Presbyterian, Episcopal, American Baptist, and others) have allowed women to serve as pastors, priests, and bishops for the past several decades.

The Church of Jesus Christ of Latter Day Saints (LDS), commonly known as the Mormons, is one of the fastest-growing religions in America and in the world. Despite such success, the Mormon Church has generated controversy on a number of issues, not the least of which is the role of women. A former president of the Church Relief Society explained the LDS view of a woman's ideal role: "A woman should give her greatest priority to her home: her husband, her family, and the opportunity for child-bearing. That is her divine mission." Some women are content with the roles set for them in Mormonism, yet not all are happy. Margaret Toscano is a University of Utah professor and *excommunicated* member of the LDS Church. In a March 2005 article in the *Deseret Morning News*, Toscano said freedom to talk about gender issues is lacking in the church. "Any woman who complains about gender equity in the church is immediately accused of being power-hungry," she said. "I know. I've been there . . . I was told to be quiet."

WOMEN'S ROLES IN NORTH AMERICAN JUDAISM TODAY

Judaism in the United States today is divided into four major religious movements represented by membership in different types of synagogues. Orthodox Judaism emphasizes the dignity and importance of women as wives and mothers. This form of Judaism does not prohibit women from pursuing careers; however, the majority of Orthodox women choose to focus their lives on family rather than education or career. Reform Judaism emphasizes ethics rather than rituals, and Reformed synagogues were the first to ordain women as rabbis. Conservative Judaism is a sort of "middle ground" between the Orthodox and Reform synagogues. Conservative Judaism originally opposed women serving as rabbis, but in recent years that has changed. The *liberal*-minded Reconstructionist movement fully supports women's equal rights.

WOMEN'S ROLES IN NORTH AMERICAN ISLAM TODAY

In an article on the Why Islam Web site, Tasleem Griffin writes: "In a time when most women were common *chattel*, the teachings of the Qur'an and the practices firmly restored to them status, both legal and social; and dignity as individuals." Griffin goes on to explain, "Not one verse in the whole of the Qur'an speaks injustice. Not one word says men and women are not equal."

Although Muslim scholars say men and women are equal in Islam, their roles are not the same. "The need of woman, in child bearing years is sustenance and security. A pregnant woman requires care; a nursing mother and infant require protection; a wife, mother, sister require respect: these are their rights." The Qur'an does state men are the stronger sex and protectors of women: "Men are the protectors and maintainers of women, because Allah has made one of them stronger than the other, and because they spend out of their possessions [to support them]" (Qur'an 4:34). In 2005, a Muslim woman named Amina Wadud defied tradition and threats and led groups of women and men in public prayer.

Women's roles in modern religion often stem from interpretations of scripture and the traditions of the religion, yet ancient traditions require critical examination. For example, all four Gospels mention Mary Magdalene, yet the traditions surrounding her have been largely mythical. At various times, church teachers have identified her as an "apostle" and teacher to the other disciples or as a prostitute. Most recently, it has been suggested she was the wife of Christ. These myths of Mary Magdalene owe more to society's views of women than to the Bible itself.

Chapter 5

MARY MAGDALENE
Disciple, Hooker, Lover?

RELIGION & MODERN CULTURE

Fictional characters Harvard professor Robert Langdon and French code expert Sophie Neveu have run to escape from the French police and from an assassin sent by Opus Dei, the Catholic religious order. They started in the Louvre Museum and then proceeded to the Swiss National Bank, picking up clues to an earth-shaking mystery. They arrive at the home of Sir Leigh Teabing, a historian who understands the secret of the Holy Grail. Teabing tells them, "The Holy Grail is Mary Magdalene . . . the mother of the royal blood line of Jesus Christ." Teabing explains that Jesus and Mary Magdalene married and she bore a child. He claims the Christian church has hidden this truth and a secret society, the Priory of Sion, passes down this secret knowledge.

Teabing further claims that Leonardo da Vinci was a member of a secret organization and revealed secret clues in his paintings.

Millions who have read Dan Brown's novel *The Da Vinci Code* are familiar with these "secrets." Due to this best-selling novel, Mary Magdalene has acquired a new identity as the wife of Jesus, a woman worthy of adoration as Goddess in the same way Christians worship Christ as God.

According to historians and scholars of art and religion, *The Da Vinci Code* is purely fiction, yet the book has focused attention on Mary Magdalene and influenced many readers' beliefs. Like Mary, the mother of Jesus, Mary Magdalene is a historical character who, through the ages, has taken on a wide variety of mythical identities.

THE MAGDALENE IN THE GOSPELS

All four Gospels of the New Testament mention Mary Magdalene. Luke informs us Mary was one of the women who traveled with Jesus and used their "resources to support Jesus and his disciples" (Luke 8:3, NLT). The same passage also tells us that Jesus had "cast out seven devils" from Mary Magdalene (8:2). When listed with other women, the Gospels place Mary Magdalene's name ahead of the others, indicating that she is the most important of the group. Mary's surname, Magdalene, indicates her town of origin, Magdala (also called Migdal), a prosperous fishing village on the shore of Lake Galilee. If she had been married, Mary's surname would have been "wife of so and so"; thus, she was single.

In the Gospels, Mary serves as witness of Jesus's death and resurrection. Matthew, Mark, and John list Magdalene first among the women who stood by the cross when Roman soldiers executed Jesus. Except for John, the male disciples were hiding from the authorities at

that time, and the women are, therefore, examples of faithfulness and courage. The Sunday after Jesus's death, Mary went to his tomb.

John chapter 20 gives Mary her starring role in history when Mary stays alone near the empty tomb, where she meets the risen Jesus. He calls her by name, "Mary!" and she replies, "Rabboni!" This is a Hebrew word that means "teacher," and is most often used when addressing God. Mary clasps Jesus, but he tells her, "Don't cling to me . . . for I haven't yet ascended to the Father. But go find my brothers and tell them that I am ascending to my Father and your Father, my God and your God." John goes on to relate how "Mary Magdalene found the disciples and told them, 'I have seen the Lord!' Then she gave them this message" (John 20:17–18, NLT).

Therefore, according to Christian tradition, Mary Magdalene is the first person entrusted with the "good news," the message of Jesus's resurrection. For this reason, preachers throughout history, including Pope John Paul II, have referred to Mary Magdalene as "the apostle to the apostles." Christians who favor women serving as priests have pointed out that a woman, Mary, was the first person in the Bible told to proclaim Jesus's message. Ernest Renan, a nineteenth-century skeptic, declared Mary to be the "inventor" of Christianity, because Renan believed Mary created the "myth" of Jesus's resurrection. Therefore, for skeptics and believers alike, Mary Magdalene plays a vital role in history.

"From the beginning her view has been ignored, unappreciated. Yet she remains. She cannot be silenced."

—*Ellen Turner, devotee to Mary Magdalene, quoted in* Time *magazine, August 11, 2003*

MARY IN THE GNOSTIC GOSPELS

Recently, scholars and religious seekers have discovered another set of Gospels, not found in the New Testament, that provide further information regarding Mary Magdalene. The Nag Hammadi Library, discovered in 1945 in Egypt, contains books with titles like the Gospel of Thomas and the Gospel of Mary. These books teach Gnosticism, a unique form of ancient Christianity. Gnostics believed that Jesus gave secret teachings to certain special followers—knowledge unknown to the writers of the Bible.

According to the Gnostic Gospels, Mary Magdalene was not only a follower of Jesus; she was the most important of his disciples. The Gospel of Philip says, "There were three who always walked with the Lord: Mary his mother and her sister and Magdalene, the one who was called his companion." In the Gospel of Mary, Peter says to her, "Sister, we know that the Savior loved you more than the rest of women. Tell us the words of the Savior which you remember—which you know but we do not, nor have we heard them." Mary Magdalene answered and said, "What is hidden from you I will proclaim to you." In these and other Gnostic Gospels, Mary Magdalene is the "smart kid" in the class, the follower of Jesus who is closer to the Lord and understands him better than the other disciples do. Thus, she becomes spiritual teacher for Jesus's male followers after his resurrection.

ANOTHER INTERPRETATION OF SOPHIA

Many theologians equate Sophia with Jesus rather than Mary Magdalene. Wisdom—Sophia—is described in the Old Testament as a feminine being who is closely identified with God. Early Christians believed these Old Testament references to Wisdom also referred to Christ, and the Gospels tell of Jesus in words that are identical to the ones used in the Old Testament to speak of Sophia; the Apostle Paul more than once refers to Christ as the Wisdom of God.

Medieval theologians had no difficulty affirming Christ's femininity. Julian of Norwich, for example, even went so far as to speak of Jesus as a "nursing mother." (For more discussion along these lines, see chapter 7.)

One Gnostic Gospel, Pistis Sophia, goes further in glorifying Mary Magdalene—it raises her to divine status. The book of Proverbs in the Hebrew Bible and Sirach in the Catholic Bible describe "Wisdom" as part of God's nature. The Gnostics believed Wisdom (*sophia* is the Greek word) was the female half of the Creator. They taught that Sophia brought evil into the world by creating humankind independent from the male deity. After seeing the destruction caused by this mistake, Sophia entered the world to try to undo the damage she had caused. In

Pistis Sophia, Mary Magdalene is not just a follower of Jesus; she is the human form of Sophia. Thus, she is the female representation of the Creator, just as Christ is the Creator's male representation on earth. Pistis Sophia is unusual among early Christian writings, portraying Mary as divine rather than merely an outstanding disciple.

According to scholars, the Gnostic Gospels tell us little about the Jesus or Mary Magdalene of history because the Gnostics wrote most of their Gospels centuries later than the New Testament Gospels. However, they do show us how many Christians in the third and fourth centuries regarded Mary Magdalene. Unlike the medieval church of the following centuries, early Christians held Mary Magdalene in high regard as a disciple and spiritual teacher.

MALE TEACHERS TRANSFORM THE DISCIPLE INTO A PROSTITUTE

On December 14, 591, Gregory "the Great" delivered a sermon to a packed congregation in Rome, the heart of medieval Christendom, that forever changed the world's understanding of Mary Magdalene. Gregory, who also Christianized England and invented Gregorian chants, declared Mary Magdalene to be the "sinful woman" who poured perfume on Jesus's feet in Luke 7:36–50. Almost immediately, other preachers identified Magdalene with the woman caught in adultery in John chapter 8 and with Mary the sister of Martha, mentioned in all the Gospels. Thus, the mythical Mary Magdalene was born—a woman created by combining four different female Bible characters into one.

Many feminists and biblical scholars today blame Gregory for ruining Mary's reputation. In the Bible, she was a faithful follower of Jesus, the first to proclaim his resurrection. In the early Church, many Christians believed she was the most spiritual and intelligent disciple, but now Christians think of her as a whore. At the time Gregory

"You have been dragged deep in the mud, but still . . . God calls to you, as He did to Zion long ago, 'Awake, awake! Thou that sittest in the dust, put on thy beautiful garments.' You can be the friend and companion of Him who came to seek and to save that which was lost. . . . Take of the very stones over which you have stumbled and fallen, and use them to pave your way to heaven."

—Josephine Butler

preached, the Catholic Church barred women from leadership and viewed women's sexuality as a temptation and threat to spirituality. Transforming the "apostle to the apostles" into a prostitute went along with those views.

Following the creation of the mythical Mary Magdalene, the legends surrounding her grew quickly. Preachers, priests, and troubadours filled in the details of her life, telling how Mary went "bad," how she met Christ and turned her life around, and how she traveled to the coast of France after Jesus's death, where she lived alone in a cave by the ocean, weeping over the sins of her former life. Mary Magdalene the restored prostitute became the most popular saint in medieval Europe, and thousands of chapels, villages, roads, hospitals, nunneries, and other sites were named after her.

Gregory's sermon ruined Mary's reputation, but medieval historians say that was not his primary intention. For Gregory, Mary the reformed prostitute was a figure of great encouragement. She was proof that no matter how bad a person's sins, she could still turn to God, receive forgiveness, and live as a saint. Thus, Mary became a powerful symbol of

THE MYTHICAL MARY GOES TO HOLLYWOOD

In the late twentieth century, Bible scholars untangled the mythical Mary from the Magdalene of history, separating the follower of Jesus from the repentant prostitute. Filmmakers, however, missed that fact. In 1973, *Jesus Christ Superstar* was popular in theaters. Yvonne Elliman played Mary Magdalene, who in the song titled "I Don't Know How to Love Him," sings, "He's a man, he's just a man, and I've had so many men before, in very many ways, he's just one more." Two decades later, Barbara Hershey played Magdalene in *The Last Temptation of Christ*. According to this film, and the novel by Nikos Kazantakis on which it was based, Mary loved Jesus but was frustrated by his choice not to marry her. Thus, she became a prostitute, explaining, "In order to forget one man . . . I've surrendered my body to men." In the television film *Jesus*, made in 1999, Debra Messing, well known from the sitcom *Will & Grace*, played Mary Magdalene, and once again, Mary was portrayed rather graphically as a prostitute. In 2004, Mel Gibson's *The Passion of the Christ* made box office history. Although the film aimed to be realistic, down to actors speaking in ancient Aramaic and Latin languages, it continued the mythical portrayal of Mary Magdalene. In Gibson's film, Monica Bellucci gave a stellar performance as Magdalene, including a flashback in which she is the woman caught in adultery. To date, only one film has portrayed Mary Magdalene in her authentic role as a follower of Jesus and witness to the resurrection, and not confused her with the "sinful woman." *The Gospel of John*, a Canadian film released in 2004, followed the Bible text word for word, thus enabling Mary to regain her historical role.

hope and divine forgiveness. This accounts for the popularity of the mythical Mary—the hooker gone good—both in the Middle Ages and in the modern age.

THE MODERN MYTH

In the twenty-first century, popular writers have recast Mary Magdalene in revised legendary form. The new Mary is equally fictitious, but more in line with modern tastes. According to *The Da Vinci Code*, Mary was the wife of Jesus and mother of his child, a daughter named Sarah. Furthermore, *The Da Vinci Code* picks up ancient Gnostic ideas and suggests Magdalene is Sophia, the divine female counterpart of Christ.

In *The Da Vinci Code*, Leigh Teabing quotes the Gnostic Gospel of Philip, "And the companion of the Savior is Mary Magdalene. Christ loved her more than all the disciples and used to kiss her often on the mouth." Teabing goes on to explain, "As any Aramaic scholar will tell you, the word *companion* in those days literally meant spouse."

Although Teabing says the Gospel of Philip is written in Aramaic, scribes wrote the Gnostic Gospels in Coptic rather than Aramaic, and in that language "companion" is an expression of spiritual kinship, not marriage. Contrary to *The Da Vinci Code*, the ancient Gnostics denied that Jesus had a physical body. Furthermore, they looked down on sex and marriage, and urged women not to marry or bear children: the Gnostics were unlikely to believe in a married Savior.

Although experts on Gnosticism and early Christianity dismiss the idea, the new mythical Mary Magdalene, the wife of Jesus, is already enshrined in popular imagination. Women in the twenty-first century no longer accept that their sexuality must be evil or a source of temptation, as the prostitute Mary suggested. As Jesus's wife, Mary Magdalene gives dignity to normal and realistic female roles: she is Jesus's best friend, sexual partner, and mate.

The Gnostic identification of Mary Magdalene as Sophia in the ancient book Pistis Sophia also fulfills modern spiritual desires. As Christ is the God-man in Christian theology, so Mary is the God-woman in Pistis Sophia, and thus the Divine Being has a female face. Of course, many modern Christians disagree with this portrayal of Magdalene as Jesus's wife and Goddess as there seems to be no basis for it in history. Instead, an increasing number of Protestants and Catholics honor Mary Magdalene for the way the Bible and early Christian writings portray her, as a model disciple and the first person to proclaim the good news of Jesus's resurrection.

Apart from her mythical roles as reformed prostitute and wife, Mary Magdalene provides a positive role for modern Christian women as an outstanding female disciple. Feminist interpreters find many such positive role models in the Bible, yet other women feel Judaism and Christianity are still religions designed for male domination. As an alternative, they revive ancient Goddess traditions.

Chapter 6

OH, MY GODDESS!

It is the night of the full moon. Nine women stand in a circle, on a rocky hill above the city. The western sky is rosy with the setting sun: in the east, the moon's face begins to peer above the horizon. . . . The woman pours out a cup of wine onto the earth, refills it and raises it high. "Hail, Tana, Mother of mothers!" she cries. "Awaken from your long sleep and return to your children again!" (From Starhawk, "Witchcraft and Women's Culture," in the book *Womanspirit Rising*.)

While many people of faith continue to worship in churches, synagogues, mosques, or temples, open-air Pagan worship like the scene described above is increasingly common in the early years of the twenty-first century.

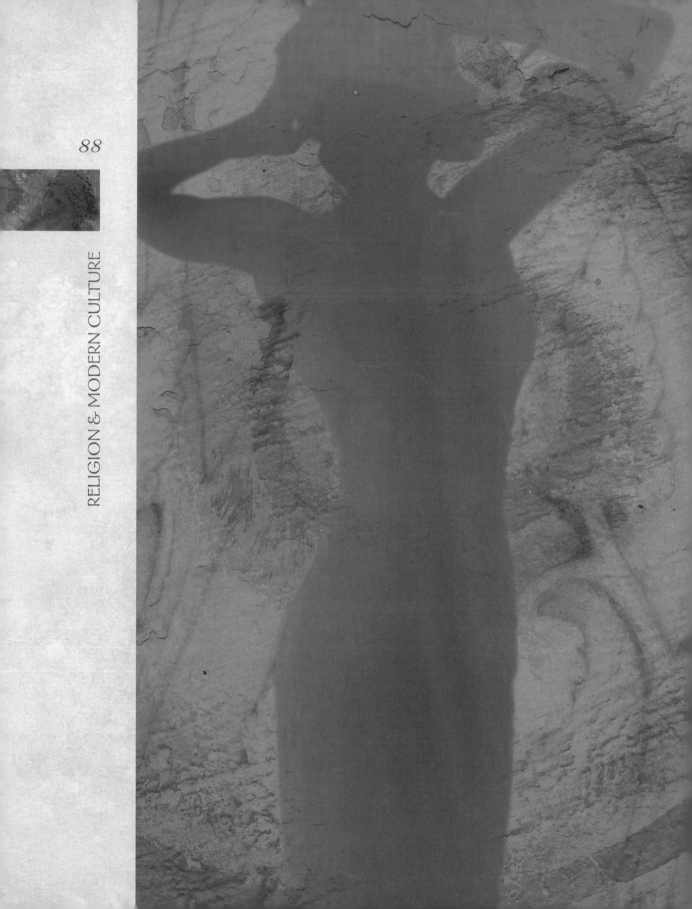

"Throughout the centuries the Goddess has acquired a thousand names and a thousand faces but most always she has represented nature, she is associated with both the sun and moon, the earth and the sky. The Goddess religion, usually in all forms, is a nature religion. Those worshipping the Goddess worship or care for nature too."

—from a Mystica online encyclopedia article titled "The Goddess"

Call it what you will—Wicca, Paganism, Neo-Paganism, Witchcraft, the Craft, or worship of the Goddess—it is a small yet rapidly growing trend in the United States and Canada. Worship of the Goddess is a combination of ancient traditions, brought back to life in new creative forms. As Starhawk, coauthor of the book *Circle Round*, puts it, Paganism today is as "primeval as the big-bellied sculptures of Paleolithic cave dwellers, modern as the thousands of Pagans linked on the Internet."

GOODBYE GOD, HELLO GODDESS

In her book *Laughter of Aphrodite*, Carol P. Christ explains why she and others find "male God symbolism of the Bible" inadequate for their spiritual needs. She says for many women, the only way to achieve a full sense of their feminine value is to leave behind the Judeo-Christian tradition and revive ancient Goddess traditions:

Goddesses are about female power. Probably that is why Goddesses have been suppressed in Western religion. This power is so threatening to the status quo that the word Goddess remains unspeakable even to many of the most radical Christian and Jewish theologians. Yet Goddess is a name that must be spoken if female power is to be acknowledged as legitimate.

Goddess worship reveres the earth and nature. In *Circle Round*, Starhawk explains:

The Earth is a living being whom we call the Goddess. Everything around us is alive and part of her living body; animals and plants, of course, but also some things that may not ordinarily seem to be alive, such as rocks, mountains, streams, rivers, stars and clouds. We also believe in many different Goddesses and Gods, whom we call by many different names. They are all spirit parts of the living universe.

Along with reverence for Mother Earth, Pagans and Wiccans honor the life-producing and nurturing physical abilities of women's bodies. As Carol Christ says:

The symbol of Goddess aids the process of naming and reclaiming the female body and its cycles and processes. In the ancient world and among modern women, the Goddess symbol represents the birth, death and rebirth processes of the natural and human worlds.

For centuries, male-dominated churches and societies told women that sexual actions, sex organs, menstruation, and pregnancy were shameful and unclean things they must hide. Goddess worshipers regard their sexual nature as sacred and glorious. Hence, many of their rituals celebrate menstruation, fertility, and birth.

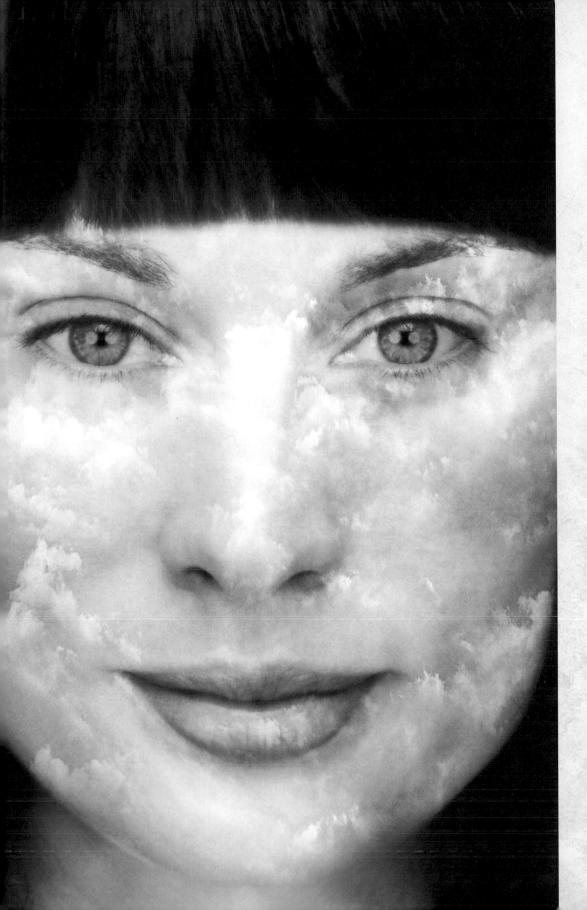

DO YOU BELIEVE IN MAGICK?

Wiccans practice magic (often spelled magick), but it does not have the amazing effects seen on television fantasy shows like *Charmed* or *Buffy the Vampire Slayer*. Starhawk describes magic as, "a way of training our imagination to make pictures and sounds and feelings and even smells in our minds that are so clear they almost seem to be real. . . . Magic can't turn straw into gold. But with magic, we can change the way we feel about things, and sometimes that can change things outside us too."

THE GODDESS WITH A THOUSAND FACES

In addition to honoring Earth and the female body, Goddess worship draws on diverse ancient traditions. The ancient Sumerians, Babylonians, Assyrians, Egyptians, Greeks, Celts, Romans, Norse, and Britons all worshipped multiple Goddesses, and various Pagan traditions today call on all of these. Especially celebrated are Gaia, the ancient Greek name for Mother Earth, and the strong and independent Diana, Goddess of the hunt, along with Aphrodite, Goddess of sexuality and love.

Modern Goddess worshippers do not simply repeat the ancient myths of the Egyptians, Greeks, or Vikings. Christian feminist

Rosemary Radford Ruether has pointed out that Goddess myths from these cultures served to exploit women. For example, the ancient Canaanite temples of Asherah required women to serve as prostitutes, and Greek myths describe male gods who rape, dominate, and banish Goddesses. However, Wiccan and Neo-Pagan worshippers say the Goddesses of the ancient world hearken back to an earlier time when the Goddess reigned and women ruled over peaceful prehistoric societies. Among the earliest human images discovered by archaeologists are the "Venus figures," nude female statues with exaggerated sexual parts that date from between 35,000 and 10,000 BCE. Archaeologist Marija Gimbutas (1921–1994) revolutionized prehistoric history in the 1970s and '80s when she claimed discovery of peace-loving, cooperation-based, Goddess-worshipping societies in Stone Age Europe. According to Gimbutas, male-dominated tribes overran these peaceful cultures. Her archaeological research has profoundly influenced modern-day feminist spirituality.

WICCA COMES OUT OF THE BROOM CLOSET

Wicca (pronounced "wik-ah") is the most popular contemporary form of Goddess worship in the United States and Canada. Female teens are the largest group of new devotees, and in the twenty-first century, an increasing number of Wiccans are coming out of the closet.

Wiccans have often been accused of devil worship, an accusation that dates back to the Middle Ages, when Goddess worshippers and herbalists were burned at the stake for this alleged crime. Wiccans adamantly deny any connection with Satanism. Dana Corby, writing on the Witches' Voice Web site, says, "Just like Christian parents, we are especially concerned about literature which links Witchcraft and Satanism. We agree with them that Satanism is not anything we want our children involved in; we just adamantly contend that it has nothing to do with us."

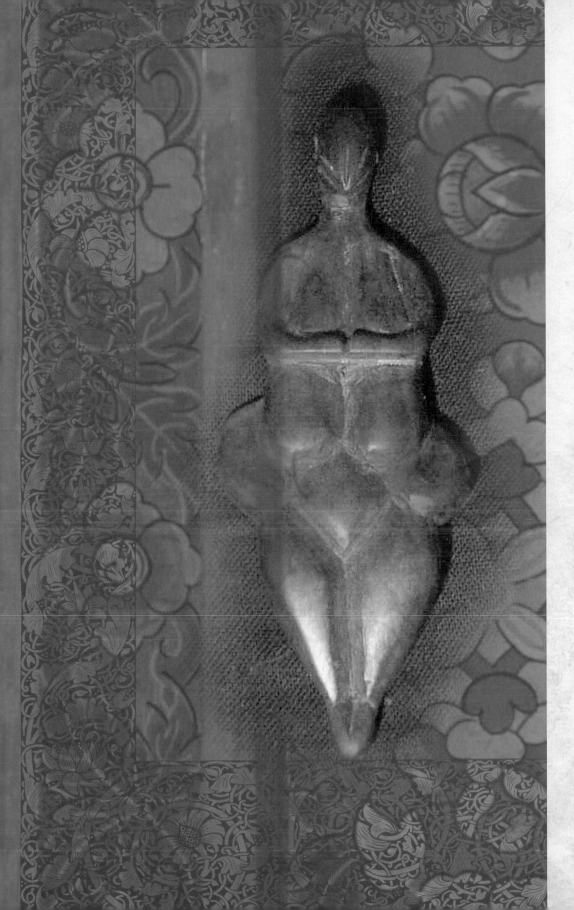

95

Wiccan practices include magick (the word is often spelled with a "k" at the end to separate it from fairy-tale magic). Working of magick usually involves ritual objects such as a magick circle, a sacred knife (Athame), a wand, or symbols of the four elements—fire, air, water and earth. The "Threefold Law of Return" governs magick, which states that any magick worked upon others will return to its originator three times as strongly. This is strong motivation to cast only positive spells.

There is one absolute moral principle in Neo-Pagan Witchcraft—the "Wiccan Rede." The Rede (Old English word for "counsel") says, "If it harms none, do as you will." In short, witches must avoid doing any sort of harm—physical, emotional, or spiritual—to others.

The Witches' Voice Web site instructs minors wanting to learn witchcraft to do so only with approval of their parents, urging teens to talk with their parents about their interest in this form of spirituality. "If your parents are still dead-set against it, you will just have to be patient." It also cautions, "Never be alone with an adult teacher." The same site says if someone offers to teach you witchcraft on the Internet, tell your parents before you begin a correspondence. "If you can't tell them, do not try to sneak around. Do not try to hide e-mail correspondence. If your parents find it one day, not only may you be in trouble, but you may have caused problems for someone else as well."

While there may be as many as half a million devotees to the Goddess or Wicca in Canada and the United States, many more people of faith continue to worship in churches, synagogues, and mosques. Some Christians are open to learning from ancient Earth religions while still retaining the essential doctrines of Christianity. Many of today's biblical scholars point out that God does not have to be worshipped as a male, since the biblical Creator has female characteristics. From this perspective, a Christian Goddess would be a viable option.

Chapter 7

DOES GOD HAVE A FEMININE SIDE?

We move through miracle days
Spirit moves in mysterious ways
She moves with it
She moves with it
Lift my days, light up my nights
—"Mysterious Ways," U2

When the immensely popular and spiritual rock band U2 released their album *Achtung Baby* in 1991, reviewers described it as an album full of songs that could be either about women or God or both. The confusion was understandable, especially since a belly dancer swirled around the band's lead singer, Bono, while he sang "Mysterious Ways" in concert (the dancer, Morleigh Steinberg, later married U2 guitarist the Edge).

RELIGION & MODERN CULTURE

"For in her is a spirit intelligent, holy, unique. . . . Firm, secure, tranquil, all-powerful, all-seeing . . . she penetrates and pervades all things. . . . For she is the . . . spotless mirror of the power of God. . . . And she, who is one, can do all things and renews everything within herself."

—Wisdom of Solomon: 7:22–27, New American Bible, describing the divine attribute of Wisdom (in Greek Sophia)

To those familiar with the Old Testament, however, "Mysterious Ways" should not have been such a mystery. Bono has said, "I've always believed that the spirit is a feminine thing." Bono's insights match the Hebrew Bible, in which the word "spirit" is indeed a feminine noun. This musical artist helped draw the world's attention to one way in which the Bible portrays God's feminine side.

While some feminists in the late twentieth century felt moved to abandon the concept of God in favor of Pagan Goddess worship, others continued to worship as Christians or Jews, reexamining the Bible for feminine images of God. Rosemary Radford Ruether, one of the most important Christian feminist theologians of the past decades, points out:

All of our human words for God are images. They are metaphors. There is no literal word that encompasses God. In fact, this is what the Hebrew tradition said was idolatry, that when we think that our one word for God is really God.

Ruether and other Christian feminists were concerned that, "When male-only language is used for God, and any feminine imagery rejected as inappropriate for God, it suggests that in some sense God is literally a male, and that only males image God and represent God."

*"The arm of a woman, in the hands of God . . .
will an earthly sovereign refuse her permission to
lead her armies?"*

—Joan of Arc

FEMALE IMAGES OF GOD IN THE BIBLE

When they sought female images of God in the Christian Old Testament, scholars came up with a number of images. In the second verse of Genesis, the Spirit (a feminine noun) "hovers" over creation, a word used to describe a female bird protecting its young in the nest. Deuteronomy 32:18 says, "You forgot the God who had given you birth" (like a mother). The prophet Isaiah said, "Can a mother forget her nursing child? Can she feel no love for a child she has borne? But even if that were possible, I would not forget you!" likening God to a mother whose love is greater than that of human mothers (Isaiah 49:15 NLT). Thirteen verses in the Old Testament describe God as mother or midwife.

Words in the Hebrew Bible also express God in a feminine manner. The common title of God, *El Shaddai*, means "God of breasts." The word *Shaddai*, breast, conveys the idea that God nourishes and satisfies his children, as a mother breastfeeds her little child. Furthermore, the Hebrew word for "compassion" is closely related to the word for "womb," thus Old Testament references to God's compassion can be translated as God's "womb-love" or "mother love."

During his earthly ministry, Jesus likened God to a woman in his teachings. Professor Ruether points out, "Jesus used feminine imagery, too. He even spoke of himself as like a mother hen wanting to gather the chicks under his wings and so on." He also compared God to a bread baker, seamstress, and housekeeper—all traditional feminine images.

103

RELIGION & MODERN CULTURE

LADY WISDOM & THE SON OF GOD

One of the most compelling female God images in the Hebrew Bible is "Lady Wisdom," found in the book of Proverbs. She is a wise woman who calls out constantly and everywhere, giving advice on the best way to live. In Proverbs, Lady Wisdom is described as co-Creator with God: "I was the architect at his side. I was his constant delight, rejoicing always in his presence" (Proverbs 8:30, NLT). In the beginning of the Gospel of John, Jesus Christ is described as the Logos, who was "with God in the beginning, through whom all things were made" (John 1:2, New International Version). Bible scholars note that Lady Wisdom and the Logos (Jesus Christ) are both described as creating the universe with God, and thus it is likely that John had Lady Wisdom in mind when describing Christ. If so, Jesus can also be thought of as a woman!

GOD & THE GODDESSES

In some churches, sermons, readings, and songs use images that express God's feminine—as well as masculine—side. However, other Christians resent the use of feminine God language, as they fear God will become confused with the Goddess. Their concerns come from interpretations of the Old Testament.

More than forty verses in the Old Testament refer to Asherah, the Canaanite fertility Goddess. All these verses are negative. Repeatedly, God's prophets warned and threatened Israel, "Stop worshipping Asherah!" Who was this female deity who so threatened Old Testament preachers? Professor and archaeologist William H. Dever, of the University of Arizona, says in an *Archaeology* magazine article, "Asherah

"You are Father, You are mother,
You are male and You are female."

—from a hymn by Synesius of Cyrene, a fifth-century Catholic bishop

was buried long ago by the Establishment: now, Archaeology has excavated her." So, who was she? According to Dever and other biblical archaeologists, "She is the wife or consort of Yahweh, the one god of Israel." In other words, she may have been yet another aspect of God, one that was suppressed by male religious leaders.

The writers of the Bible, a group that Carol P. Christ refers to as the "Yahweh only" camp, had zero tolerance for Israel worshipping the Goddess alongside God. Why were they so opposed? Many modern feminists believe that Asherah empowered women and the priests of Yahweh put down worship of the Goddess to keep women in submission. Yet the Bible itself and some biblical archaeologists argue that worship of Asherah did women more harm than good, since Asherah religion required women to serve as "sacred" prostitutes. A religion that glorifies women as sex objects does not truly affirm women's equality.

Despite these conflicting viewpoints, at the beginning of the twenty-first century, many people of faith would disagree with C. S. Lewis, the famous Christian writer of the previous century, who believed God is "so masculine, we are all feminine in relation to him." More people side with Margo Houts, adjunct professor at San Francisco Theological Seminary and Fuller Theological Seminary, who says, "Let us also affirm the consistent witness of the church, namely, that God is neither feminine nor masculine . . . neither male nor female." Today, women's influence in religion is changing how we understand sex roles, church rites, and even how we understand the divine.

DOES GOD HAVE A FEMININE SIDE?

Brown, Dan. *The Da Vinci Code*. New York: Random House, 2003.

Deen, Edith. *All of the Women of the Bible*. New York: HarperSanFrancisco, 1988.

Evans, Mary. *Woman in the Bible*. Carlisle, Cumbria: Paternoster, 1998.

Evans, Mary, and Catherine Clark Kroeger. *The IVP Women's Bible Commentary*. Downers Grove, Ill.: InterVarsity Press, 2002.

Grady, J. Lee. *10 Lies the Church Tells Women*. Lake Mary, Fla.: Charisma House, 2002.

Grady, J. Lee. *25 Tough Questions About Women and the Church*. Lake Mary, Fla.: Charisma House, 2003.

Hahn, Scott. *Hail, Holy Queen: The Mother of God in the Word of God*. New York: Doubleday, 2001.

Liefeld, Walter, and Ruth A. Tucker. *Daughters of the Church: Women and Ministry from New Testament Times to the Present*. Grand Rapids, Mich.: Zondervan, 1987.

Starbird, Margaret. *The Goddess in the Gospels: Reclaiming the Sacred Feminine*. Santa Fe, N.M.: Bear & Company, 1998.

Torjesen, Karen Jo. *When Women Were Priests: Women's Leadership in the Early Church & the Scandal of Their Subordination in the Rise of Christianity*. New York: HarperSanFrancisco, 1993.

FOR MORE INFORMATION

Christians for Biblical Equality
www.cbeinternational.org

Is God Masculine?
www.touchstonemag.com/docs/
issues/16.1docs/16-1pg41.html

The Mary Page
www.udayton.edu/mary/
marypage21.html

Mary Magdalene in Wikipedia
the Free Encyclopedia
en.wikipedia.org/wiki/
Mary_Magdalene

The Pagan Library
www.paganlibrary.com

Starhawk's Home Page
www.starhawk.org

Z Budapest's Website
www.zbudapest.com

What the Bible says about
Women's Ordination
www.religioustolerance.org/
ord_bibl.htm

The Witches Voice
www.witchvox.com

Publisher's note:
The Web sites listed on this page were active at the time of publication.
The publisher is not responsible for Web sites that have changed their
addresses or discontinued operation since the date of publication. The
publisher will review and update the Web-site list upon each reprint.

PICTURE CREDITS

The illustrations in RELIGION AND MODERN CULTURE are photo montages made by Dianne Hodack. They are a combination of her original mixed-media paintings and collages, the photography of Benjamin Stewart, various historical public-domain artwork, and other royalty-free photography collections.

AUTHOR: Kenneth McIntosh is a freelance writer living in Flagstaff, Arizona, with his wife, Marsha, and two teen children, Jonathan and Eirené. Kenneth has a bachelor's degree in English and a master's degree in theology. He is the author of two dozen books, including *Women in North America's Religions* and *Lost Gospels and Hidden Codes: New Concepts of Scripture*. He enjoys hiking, boogie boarding, and vintage Volkswagens. He formerly spent a decade teaching junior high in inner-city Los Angeles, another decade serving as an ordained minister, and is currently founding a new church, The Journey.

CONSULTANT: Dr. Marcus J. Borg is the Hundere Distinguished Professor of Religion and Culture in the Philosophy Department at Oregon State University. Dr. Borg is past president of the Anglican Association of Biblical Scholars. Internationally known as a biblical and Jesus scholar, the *New York Times* called him "a leading figure among this generation of Jesus scholars." He is the author of twelve books, which have been translated into eight languages. Among them are *The Heart of Christianity: Rediscovering a Life of Faith* (2003) and *Meeting Jesus Again for the First Time* (1994), the best-selling book by a contemporary Jesus scholar.

CONSULTANT: Dr. Robert K. Johnston is Professor of Theology and Culture at Fuller Theological Seminary in Pasadena, California, having served previously as Provost of North Park University and as a faculty member of Western Kentucky University. The author or editor of thirteen books and twenty-five book chapters (including *The Christian at Play*, 1983; *The Variety of American Evangelicalism*, 1991; *Reel Spirituality: Theology and Film in Dialogue*, 2000; *Life Is Not Work/Work Is Not Life: Simple Reminders for Finding Balance in a 24/7 World*, 2000; *Finding God in the Movies: 33 Films of Reel Faith*, 2004; and *Useless Beauty: Ecclesiastes Through the Lens of Contemporary Film*, 2004), Johnston is the immediate past president of the American Theological Society, an ordained Protestant minister, and an avid bodysurfer.